W9-CEX-434

"This book really shows that everyone has a talent, even if they don't know what it is yet. Sometimes to find it, you have to use a little bit of teamwork."
Dolly, age 8

"One of the best books I've ever read."
Meg, age 7

"I love this adventure! It's made me want to save the world, just like Katy, Cassie, and Zia!"
Annabel, age 6

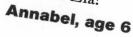

"This is a really fun and magical story, and the characters really remind me of my best friends."
Eloise, age 8

Katy

Chatty, sociable, and kind. She's the glue that holds the Playdate Adventure Club together. Likes animals (especially cats) and has big dreams of saving the world one day.

Cassie

Shy but brave when she needs to be. She relies on her friends to give her confidence. Loves dancing, especially street dance, but only in the privacy of her bedroom.

Zia

Loud, confident, and intrepid. She's a born leader but can sometimes get carried away. Likes schoolwork and wants to be a scientist when she's older, just like her mom.

Thunder

Big, white, and fluffy with gray ears, paws, and tail. He's blind in one eye, but that's what makes him extra special. Likes chasing mice, climbing trees, and going on adventures. Is also a cat.

**Join Katy, Cassie, and Zia
on more Playdate Adventures**

The Wishing Star
The Magic Ocean Slide
The Giant Chestnut

THE NORTH POLE PICNIC

★ THE PLAYDATE ★
ADVENTURES

KATY   ZIA   CASSIE

THUNDER

THE
NORTH POLE
PICNIC

Emma Beswetherick

Illustrated by Anna Woodbine

ROCK THE BOAT

A Rock the Boat Book

First published by Rock the Boat,
an imprint of Oneworld Publications, 2020

ISBN 978-1-78607-871-1
ISBN 978-1-78607-966-4 (ebook)

Printed and bound in Great Britain by Clays Ltd, Elcograf S.p.A.

Oneworld Publications
10 Bloomsbury Street, London, WC1B 3SR, England

Stay up to date with the latest books,
special offers, and exclusive content from
Rock the Boat with our newsletter

Sign up on our website
oneworld-publications.com/rtb

To my family,
who love vacations in the snow

CHAPTER ONE

❄ ❄ ❄ ❄ ❄ ❄ ❄ ❄ ❄

Zia LOVED the Christmas vacation. Her family were Muslim and celebrated a festival called Eid twice each year, but this was still a special time for them. They loved the twinkling lights that brightened up the town, and even though they didn't exchange presents like the families of lots of children in her class, they spent time seeing aunts, uncles, and cousins, and eating lots of delicious food. This year was going to be even more special because in just a few days they were flying to India for a family wedding. But before that Zia had the last day of term to enjoy, and it was going to be AWESOME for two AWESOME reasons. Firstly, because her best friends were coming for a playdate after school. Secondly, because it was a non-school-uniform day. Put these things together and it meant today was definitely going to be Zia's favorite day of the entire term.

"Come *on*, Zia! It's time to leave!" yelled her mom. Zia's family was a loud, bellowy sort of family. "Your sisters are waiting!"

Zia wondered how many times she'd been called already—her mind had been too occupied with playdates and choosing what to wear to notice. "Coming, coming!" she bellowed back from her room, checking her silver leggings and fluffy turquoise sweater in the mirror one last time. "Have you found my light-up sneakers?"

"Yes! You know you've asked me that about

five times already this morning?" Her mom had that half-cross face she often wore in the mornings before school—somewhere between a frown and a grin.

Zia trotted down the stairs, then smiled innocently at her mom while she put on her sneakers. Her older sisters were fighting (as usual) to see who could get their coats down from the peg first.

"Everyone ready?" their mom asked, hurrying them out of the door so as not to be late for the bell. "And remember," she said, turning to Zia, "your friends are coming for a playdate after school."

Zia's heart did another little leap of excitement.

"Mom, you know I've told *you* that about five times this morning!" she said cheekily. Surely her mom knew that was one thing she couldn't possibly forget.

Zia was in Junipers class at Bishop's Park Primary (every class in her year was named after a tree or shrub) along with her two best friends, Cassandra and Katy. The three girls were inseparable and loved nothing more than planning adventures—and going on playdates to each other's houses. Last term they'd set up a new secret club called the Playdate Adventure Club and it was the coolest thing Zia had ever been a part of.

That lunchtime, after finishing off the calendars they'd been making in class, the three girls huddled in the cold playground, chatting excitedly about the playdate they were having later.

"I've told my sisters they're not allowed in my room the whole time we're playing!" Zia exclaimed.

"Good thinking." Katy smiled—she didn't have brothers or sisters so didn't have the same kind of problems Zia had with hers. Zia loved her sisters a lot, especially when they helped her with her homework, but sometimes they could be way too naughty.

"Do you think that thing might happen again at your house today, Zia?" Cassandra whispered.

Katy looked nervously over her shoulder, not wanting them to be heard by the other children in the playground. "You mean the same thing that happened when we had a playdate at my house?"

Cassandra nodded.

"I hope so," said Zia.

But they didn't get to finish their conversation because the bell went for them to line up in the playground, ready for afternoon class.

For the rest of the school day Zia couldn't get the playdate out of her head. Something *amazing* had happened at Katy's house last time. It was as though some kind of magic had descended on them all and turned their pretend adventure to space into an *actual real space mission.* Now Zia couldn't wait to get home to find out whether the same thing was going to happen today.

"Zia, are you with us?" Ms. Coco asked impatiently. Their teacher had walked over to

Zia's desk and was now leaning her hands on the table. Zia *always* worked hard and never usually found it difficult to concentrate.

"Um, yes, sorry," she gulped, letting go of her braid and sitting up straight to make it look as though she was paying attention.

Ms Coco made a disbelieving "hmmmm" sound and walked back to the whiteboard.

That was close, Zia thought, feeling Katy and Cassandra's eyes on her.

She dared one more glance at the clock on the classroom wall.

Only forty-five minutes left of the school day, and then they'd be able to find out.

CHAPTER TWO

❄ ❄ ❄ ❄ ❄ ❄ ❄ ❄ ❄ ❄

RIIIIIIIIIIIIIIIIIIIIIIIIIIIIIIIIIIIIIIIIIIIIIIING!

As soon as the bell went, and as soon as Ms. Coco said it was OK to do so, the girls jumped out of their seats to grab their coats and bags. They were first into the playground, where crowds of grown-ups were waiting patiently in the cold.

"Ms. Coco, I can see my mom," Zia cried, arm stretched high in the air.

"OK, girls, off you go. And have fun!" their teacher said, smiling.

"You too, Ms. Coco. Merry Christmas!" they replied, then they turned to each other and grinned.

"PLAYDATE, PLAYDATE, LET'S GO ON A PLAYDATE," they chanted, as they bustled past Zia's mom and her two sisters in their rush to leave the school gates. Zia held onto her friends' hands and pulled them along in the icy December air, racing toward her house. She was so desperate to get home she didn't want to waste even a second!

Reaching the front door, the girls burst into the hall in a messy heap of coats, hats, scarves, and school bags. Zia then dragged them up the stairs and across the landing to her bedroom. "This way," she wheezed—she felt quite out of breath after all that running—and jostled them inside. They stood catching their breath until eventually Katy and Cassandra's eyes began to circle around the room, taking everything in.

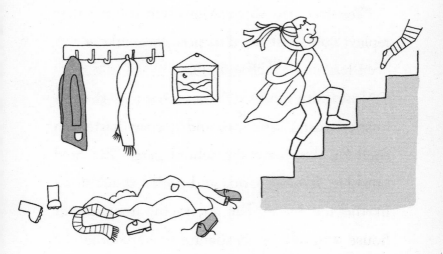

"So, I've been thinking," said Zia, eager to start planning their adventure. "How about we go somewhere cold and wintry this time?"

Katy and Cassandra were looking out of the window, where tiny flecks of snow were beginning to fall.

"Yes, I love the snow!" exclaimed Katy.

"Only if it's not *too* cold," said Cassandra. Cassandra was always a little unsure about things at first.

11

"Cassie!" said Zia exasperatedly. "Snow is *always* cold. But it's also precious—like we've been learning at school."

Cassandra smiled, then nodded as though remembering. This term Ms. Coco had been teaching them about climate change and how precious habitats are in serious trouble all around the world. The poster Zia made about Arctic animals losing their homes because of melting ice caps had been shown in assembly that week at school.

"I just thought it would be awesome to visit the Arctic for real," Zia went on. "We might even meet some of the animals."

"That would be so cool!" Katy grinned, her green eyes glinting. "I'd love to meet an Arctic hare."

"And I've always wanted to see what the North Pole looks like," said Cassandra, starting to warm to the idea.

12

"You know what I'd love?" continued Zia. "It might sound crazy, but I thought we could have a picnic there. Not a picnic in the park, like we do in summer. But an icy cold picnic. A North Pole picnic!"

"Yes!" exclaimed Katy enthusiastically. "And we could eat lots of icy treats decorated with snowy white frosting."

"On an icy white blanket that glitters in the sunlight!" Cassandra beamed, completely on board with their plan at last.

But before they could make preparations for their snowy adventure, they heard a noise coming from outside.

"W-w-w-what is that?" asked Cassandra, her freckly face turning pale.

They tiptoed over to the bedroom window

and stared into the darkening street, little puffs of hot breath steaming up the glass. The air looked misty with falling snow, light from the streetlamps creating an eerie glow across the sidewalks. Then they heard the sound again—and shivered.

"Look, down there! I can see something moving!" shouted Katy.

A ghostly shape was slinking its way toward the house. It stopped right under Zia's window, stared straight up at them with one blue eye and meowed.

"THUNDER!" they all shouted.

"Katy, is that really your cat?" Cassandra said with surprise and relief.

"Yes, I'd know him anywhere!" Katy replied. Thunder was a ragdoll rescue cat and had lost one of his eyes in a fight. Apparently (according to Katy's dad) it made him extra special. "I told him I was going to your house today, Zia. I hoped he'd come, but I didn't think he actually *would*!"

The girls charged out of Zia's bedroom, down the stairs to the front door and peered into the

freezing gloom. Thunder was sitting on top of the bike shed, smiling in the superior way that cats do, his creamy fur glowing ghost-like in the twilight.

"What are you doing sitting up there, silly? We've come to sneak you inside," Katy said, walking out into the snow and opening her arms wide. Thunder stared at Katy and then sort of rolled off the top of the shed—he was quite a fat cat—straight into her arms.

She hoisted him up higher so he was sitting snuggly in her arms and, following the others, staggered as quickly as she could into the house. They were back in Zia's bedroom, leaning against the closed door and panting, before Zia's mom knew anything had happened.

"Right, we should get started," Zia said.

Katy plonked Thunder on the floor and Cassandra began to fuss over him, stroking his damp fur, and nuzzling his neck with kisses. Thunder mewed a few times and brushed himself against her ankles, then slunk over to the corner, where he casually flopped onto the carpet.

"Come on, how about I get some white sheets and we turn my room into the Arctic? You two find as many Arctic cuddly toys as you can. I know I have a killer whale somewhere—I got it when my sisters adopted one for my birthday last year."

Zia disappeared outside her room and tiptoed toward the big linen closet on the landing. When she appeared again, arms laden with spare bedding, she found her friends waiting with several toys seated around the edge of the room. They all got to work, draping white sheets and duvet covers over the floor and furniture until Zia's room had been transformed into a winter wonderland. Then they stood back and smiled.

"It looks AMAZING!" Cassandra cried proudly.

"It does, doesn't it?" squealed Katy.

"Just a few more things and we'll be ready," said Zia. "We should pack a bag of provisions. Some snacks—obviously—and some clothes we might need. Hats, scarves, gloves, warm undershirts, and leggings. That kind of thing!" She rummaged in a drawer next to her bed until she found some chocolate bars and a pack of candy she had left over from a party bag, then opened her closet and pulled out some winter clothes and accessories.

"There, I think that's everything. Cassie, can you pass me those bags in the corner?"

Cassie handed Zia two small rucksacks and the girls worked together, stuffing them full with everything they might need for their adventure.

When they'd finished, Zia beamed at her friends. "So, who's ready to go to the North Pole?"

CHAPTER THREE

❄ ❄ ❄ ❄ ❄ ❄ ❄ ❄ ❄

On their last playdate, Zia, Katy, and Cassandra had decided to mark the beginning of their adventure by standing in a circle and reciting a sort of password. They got into the same position, with Thunder in the middle, and grabbed each other's hands in a tight squeeze.

"Now, close your eyes and imagine yourself in the Arctic," Zia instructed, trying to calm the butterflies in her tummy. "The North Pole is towering into the sky and all around is fluffy white snow as far as your eyes can see!"

"Um, you know the North Pole isn't a *real* pole," interrupted Katy.

Zia grinned. "Of course, silly! But it's more fun to imagine it is. How else will we know we're in the right place?"

"Good point," said Katy. "Ignore me!" She laughed.

"OK, now repeat after me," Zia continued. "I wish to go on an adventure."

"*I wish to go on an adventure,*" the girls chanted in unison, all eyes scrunched closed.

After just a few seconds, they started to have the same fizzy, bubbly sensation they'd had at Katy's house. They felt both BOILING hot and FREEZING cold, as if their bodies were super-charging with electricity. And then, as quickly as the peculiar sensations had started, they stopped. Everyone slowly opened their eyes.

"OH!" exclaimed Katy.

"MY!" gasped Cassandra.

"GOODNESS!" cried Zia. Katy and Cassandra put their arms around her, and they turned slowly in a circle, taking in their surroundings.

They were no longer standing in Zia's bedroom among white cotton sheets, but on actual, real snow—the kind that looked like whipped cream rather than the wet, muddy stuff they got at home. All about them was gleaming white for miles and miles, with icy cliffs towering up into a clear blue sky to their right and silky white terrain stretching all the way to their front and left.

Then Zia looked down and gasped again, because rather than their own clothes, they were now wearing thick coats with furry hoods, expedition pants, and big, padded snow boots and gloves. They looked like *real* Arctic explorers!

"I can't believe it's happened again!" Zia shrieked. She linked arms with Katy and Cassandra excitedly, and soon the three of them were picking up armfuls of snow and throwing it in every direction.

"I've never seen so much snow in my life!" Katy exclaimed, taking aim at the back of Zia's head. "I mean, we're actually in the Arctic!" *Bullseye!* The snowball exploded on Zia's hood.

Zia made a snowball and hurled it back at Katy, then Cassandra joined in and soon the three girls were laughing so much their sides began to hurt.

"OK," Zia blurted out eventually, trying to brush off her giggles as she also brushed the snow from her coat and hood. "We can't

stand around having a snowball fight all day."
She took one more snowball to the face and
squealed. "Come on, we need to find our way
to the North Pole."

They stared into the distance, straining their
eyes in search of a clue as to which way they
should go.

"Um, guys, look over there," said Cassandra
timidly. "Is that what I think it is?"

Zia looked in the direction Cassandra was
pointing with her gloved hand and that's when
she saw it, a thin, icy-blue pole some way off in
the distance, soaring up, up, up into the sky.

"Cassandra!" cried Zia enthusiastically.
"You found it! That *must* be the
North Pole!"

She was about to start heading
toward it when Katy put up her hands
to stop her.

"Hold on a minute. Where's Thunder?" Katy asked, looking worried.

Their eyes scoured the ground, but Thunder was nowhere to be seen...until, moments later, two small gray ears began to emerge from the snow, followed by a gray-and-white face with frosted whiskers, a green hooded coat, and finally four paws and a bushy gray tail.

"Thunder!" the girls shouted, relieved.

"Look at you!" said Katy, trying hard to stifle

a giggle. "You're all covered in snow!"

"What else would I be covered in?" he replied in a cross voice.

Zia had forgotten that Thunder had been able to speak on their last adventure. She wondered if she'd ever get used to hearing animals talk.

"I hate the cold," the cat continued, licking his paws and wiping his whiskers.

"Oh, don't be a spoilsport," said Katy, heaving the cat into her arms, brushing the snow from his coat and putting him back down. "It's going to be fun. You'll see."

"Fine," said the cat. "Just don't expect me to like it."

With a smile, Katy started walking towards the icy pole. "Who's coming?" she said, Thunder trotting, with difficulty, by her feet. Cassandra and Zia followed close behind.

They couldn't go fast. It was quite exhausting walking through thick snow. With every step their boots sunk a bit deeper and they had to use all their effort to pull them back up again. They trudged forwards like this for ages, mostly in silence, and without seeing any signs of life around them. But just as Zia was about to open her mouth to suggest they take a rest, she noticed something up ahead, something big and white and furry. As they got closer, she realised what it was. She didn't like it, not one little bit.

"Polar bear!" she shouted. "Everyone, RUN!"

CHAPTER FOUR

❄ ❄ ❄ ❄ ❄ ❄ ❄ ❄ ❄

Even though they'd come to the North Pole in search of animals, the sight of a real polar bear filled them with dread. Zia had been told at school that they were the deadliest animals in the Arctic. Now she was faced with one, she didn't want to stick around to find out if that was true.

"But I thought we were here to *see* the animals," yelled Katy, as the four explorers turned and ran for their lives. Zia grabbed Cassandra's hand, Cassandra grabbed Katy's,

Katy swept Thunder up under her free arm and now Zia was dragging them all away as fast as she could in the snow.

"I know, but polar bears *eat* humans, Katy!" exclaimed Zia desperately. "Didn't you hear what Ms. Coco said? *Polar bears are the only animals that hunt humans for food.* Do you really want to become its dinner?"

"No, I...I guess you're right," Katy replied fearfully.

"I *am* right, so—"

"STOP!"

A deep voice boomed across the snow and halted the girls in their tracks.

"DON'T GO ANY FURTHER. I'M WARNING YOU. STAY WHERE YOU ARE."

Zia pulled the others toward her, remembering there was safety in numbers.

Then they turned around together so they were facing the bear.

"W-w-what do you think it w-wants?" stammered Cassandra.

"I hope it's not hungry." Katy trembled.

"Perhaps I should do the talking," said

33

Thunder, with an air of confidence. "You know, animal to animal."

"Ummmm, I'm not sure that's such a good idea," said Katy.

"We don't want to anger the bear anymore than we have already," added Cassandra, nervously eyeing the approaching animal.

The polar bear lumbered toward them until it was so close Zia could smell the fishiness on its stale breath. Her stomach churned.

"I'm Pilar, Queen and Ruler of the Frozen Lands. Humans aren't welcome here. It is because of humans that our homeland is being destroyed. And, worse than that, you've come at a sacred time, in the middle of our festivities. You should go back to where you came from."

The bear's voice was so loud they could feel the ground shaking beneath them. They all took a step back—except Thunder, who jumped out of Katy's arms and bravely crept a little closer.

"If I may," the cat said, bowing his head respectfully to the enormous creature, "I'd kindly ask that you don't scare my friends like that."

The bear let out a fierce growl that echoed around them and Zia could see bits of flesh hanging from its teeth. However helpful Thunder thought he was being, it clearly wasn't working.

"What I think our cat means to say, madam," Zia began, her knees shaking and her heart pounding in her chest, "is that we're sorry if we've offended you. We didn't mean to intrude and we're certainly not here to destroy your homeland." She stepped in front of Thunder to shield him from the bear. "We're on an adventure, and we'd really like to meet the Arctic animals, if you'll introduce us."

The bear roared with laughter so that the ground shook around them again.

"You want to join our festivities? A cat and *three humans!*" Pilar reared up on her back feet, front paws clawing at her tummy as she continued to laugh. "Let's see what the others have to say about that. Follow me," she said, landing back on all fours with another growl.

Zia hesitated. She had no idea what they had invited themselves to, but she didn't want to anger Pilar more by asking questions.

"I said, FOLLOW ME!" bellowed the bear. She turned and plodded away.

The girls and Thunder set off after her, finding it difficult to keep up, even though Pilar went slowly. Her wide, padded paws made perfect snowshoes, whereas they weren't used to wearing such big, heavy boots. Every now and then Pilar turned around to check

they were all still following, until, after what seemed like a lifetime, she stopped in front of the tallest archway Zia had ever seen, with ice walls stretching far out on either side.

"The others are just through there," Pilar told them, pointing at the arch. It was made from intricately carved ice of a shimmering pale blue that glittered like diamonds.

"We have to go in th-th-there?" whispered Cassandra uneasily. "What's on the other side?"

"You'll see," said the bear, grinning curiously. She plodded toward the arch, beckoning the girls to follow.

Everyone held hands as they walked slowly forward, stretching their necks back and looking up at the towering sculpture of ice above them. When they reached the other side, they stood frozen to the spot, taking in the incredible sight before them. The archway

opened onto the most enormous stadium
Zia had ever seen, built
of the same glittering
blue ice. And right in
the middle of the arena,
stretching higher even
than the archway
itself, was the towering
ice pole they'd seen
from afar when they'd
first arrived on their
adventure.

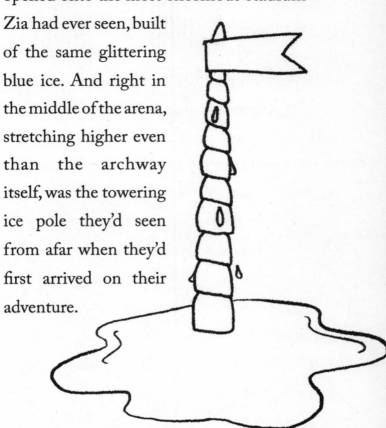

They'd made it at last—the North Pole.

CHAPTER FIVE

❄ ❄ ❄ ❄ ❄ ❄ ❄ ❄

The girls' eyes were fixed on the pole in front of them, so they didn't notice at first that thousands of other eyes were fixed on them. Every seat around the arena was occupied by an animal of some kind—there were polar bears, whales, narwhals, dolphins, seals, walruses, foxes, wolves, hares, reindeer, puffins, and hundreds of other birds—and now they were roaring and growling and mocking and jeering as loudly as they could.

"They clearly don't like humans," Zia whispered to her friends.

"I wonder what we've done wrong?" whispered Katy in return. Cassandra just stared ahead, eyes wide with fright.

They continued to follow Pilar toward the center of the arena, conscious now of their audience, until the bear finally stopped in front of a grand podium of ice built around the base of the pole. On it sat a walrus, a wolf, and an eagle, each looking down regally from ornate thrones carved out of the same sparkling blue ice. Pilar leapt onto the podium and took her place on the biggest and grandest throne of them all before beginning to speak.

"Council, I have brought you three humans and their cat," she bellowed. "They say they want to join us today—that it is part of an *adventure*. But we all know humans are to blame for our homeland being destroyed. Should we trust them? Or should we send them back to where they came from?" she growled.

The council of animals walked over to Pilar, bowing their heads together so the girls couldn't hear what they were saying. Then they returned to their thrones and Pilar once again spoke so that even the animals at the back of the stadium could hear her.

"The council wish me to explain something to our visitors. Come!" she said, summoning them up onto the raised platform.

They joined Pilar on the icy podium, careful not to slip, and approached the middle, where the magnificent North Pole soared upward into the crystal-clear blue sky. Around the base of the pole was a pool of water, and the lower part of the pole was a different texture to the rest. It was softer-looking, less shiny. Zia was shocked to realize the pole was melting.

"As I said before, you've arrived at a sacred time," Pilar told them. "Every year we come together in celebration of the Arctic by hosting three days of sport. We also use this time to honor our magnificent North Pole, the symbol of our homeland, but a symbol that, sadly, is slowly being destroyed. As you can see, the pole is melting, and each year this pool of water gets bigger. *This* is why we don't trust you. Humans have caused the Great Melt to happen. Why should we trust you now?"

Katy and Cassandra looked as shocked and saddened by what they saw as Zia. None of them spoke—no one knew what to say—but they felt an enormous responsibility to make things right.

Zia took a step forward. "I…I…I'm sorry the Arctic is melting," she said, with more courage than she was feeling. "We've learned

about climate change at school. Seeing it for real makes us sad. But before we answer your question, could we have a moment to talk?"

"I'll give you two minutes," said the bear gruffly, going back to her throne.

"What do you think?" asked Zia, when there was no longer a chance of being heard. "What should we say?"

Cassandra fiddled with her hood in concentration and Katy held Thunder tightly in her arms.

"I don't think it's fair the animals blame you for the North Pole melting," said Thunder haughtily. "Humans have a lot to answer for, but it's hardly the fault of three girls!"

"I agree," said Katy, rubbing Thunder behind the ears in gratitude. "How can the animals blame us? What have we done to harm them?"

"I don't think they're actually blaming *us*," said Cassandra thoughtfully. "But they *are* blaming humans. Do you remember in class when Ms. Coco asked us to list all the things that have caused climate change to happen? Every one of them is caused by humans!"

Zia looked at her friend, and it dawned on her what they needed to do. "Cassie, you're magnificent! That's the answer, surely? We tell Pilar we'd like to learn more about the Arctic, and in return we'll promise to take our knowledge home and share it with our friends. If we understand more about their way of living and how their habitat is being destroyed, we'll also have a greater understanding of why they need our help. What do you think?"

"I think it's worth a try," agreed Cassandra.

"Yes, nice one, Cassie!" said Katy, patting her

47

friend on the shoulder.

When the two minutes were up, Pilar returned. "Well," she barked, "what do you have to say?"

This time Cassandra, encouraged by her friends, took a tentative step forward and began to tell the bear nervously what they'd just discussed.

"S-s-so, you see, if you would just let us stay and watch your winter games—*a-a-and* join your celebration," she stuttered, "w-we'll be able to learn more about your homeland and understand why humans need to do more to protect it."

Zia and Katy stood by Cassandra's side for support, and Pilar glared at them intensely before returning to her throne to consult with her council. Then, after a few more moments, she summoned them to come and stand before her.

"This is our deal," she bellowed, again so all the animals in the arena could hear. "You can stay, but under these terms. One, you each enter one of today's events. Two, at least one of you must win an event to join in our festivities. If you lose all your games, you go straight home."

Zia looked at her friends to see whether they agreed with the deal. Katy and Thunder nodded reluctantly. Cassandra shrugged, her face pale.

"You have a deal," she said meekly.

A sudden cheer broke from the crowd, like a clap of thunder.

Pilar nodded. "Let the games begin!" she announced, finally cracking a smile.

CHAPTER SIX

❋ ❋ ❋ ❋ ❋ ❋ ❋ ❋ ❋

The animals had already hosted two days of sport so today was the final day of the winter games. They were starting with the high jump, followed by the 100-meter swim, and concluding with a weightlifting competition. A group of hares was warming up in one corner of the arena, ready to start the first event.

"Thunder, why don't you compete in the first game?" Katy encouraged him. "Cats are great at jumping. You'd stand a better chance of beating those hares than any of us."

Thunder grinned. "I'd be honored to. But don't you think one of you should compete as well?"

"Thunder's right," said Cassandra. "There are three events, and we *all* have to join in at least one." Her freckly face had turned pale.

"OK, well, I'm happy to do the high jump with Thunder," offered Katy. "I love gymnastics and that involves *some* jumping. Cassie, how about you do the swimming race? You're best in the year—and Zia, you're really strong. Perhaps you do the weightlifting?"

"Agreed," said Zia. "Excellent plan. Cassie, is that OK with you?"

Cassandra slowly nodded her head.

Pilar pointed to where a long, thin ice pole was balanced at either end upon stacks of ice, a mound of fluffy white snow piled behind it for contestants to land on. A loud whistle echoed around the stadium and Katy and Thunder said hasty goodbyes before rushing over to it, while Cassandra and Zia were ushered to their seats.

"Do you think they'll be OK?" asked Cassandra, as an Arctic hare with the number 98 printed on its vest took up position.

"I hope so," replied Zia, feeling nervous for her friends and crossing her fingers tightly by her side.

Three hares attempted the jump first. Each competitor had just one chance to get over the pole. If they failed,  they would be out of the competition. If they cleared it, they'd go through to the next round, when the pole would be raised higher.

"GOOD LUCK, THUNDER!" Zia and Cassandra shouted from their seats.

Thunder was nervous—running and jumping

on ice and snow wasn't the same as hurdling fences back home. He started his run-up, and Zia and Cassandra gasped as his feet skidded out. But then he took off and cleared the pole by a whisker.

"AMAZING WORK, THUNDER!" the girls shouted.

Next it was Katy's turn. Human legs aren't as well designed for jumping, and her boots and winter clothes were cumbersome. The slippery

ice didn't help either, but she managed to launch herself into the air and over—just!—brushing the pole and leaving it wobbling as she disappeared into the deep snow on the other side.

"YEEEEEEEEEEEES, KATY!" Zia and Cassandra both screamed.

Round two, and again the hares sprung skillfully over the ice pole. The crowd went wild but quietened when Thunder got into position.

Zia felt Cassandra grab her hand anxiously as he sprinted forward. But this time he made a good run-up and cleared the pole easily before tumbling into the crash mat of snow.

"Go, Thunder!" they cried.

Now it was Katy, who looked more nervous. She started to run but misjudged the height of the pole, and as she landed in the deep snow on the other side, it toppled down after her. Zia

felt her heart sink and Cassandra gasped beside her. Katy was out, but at least Thunder was still in the competition.

The pole was now set at its most challenging height, and only the third hare cleared it this time—by the tiniest of margins. The crowd erupted into cheers, but once again went quiet as Thunder readied himself. It was all down to this final jump.

Thunder ran, skidded, jumped, but this time knocked the pole clean off the icy frame before landing.

"NO!" Zia and Cassandra gasped from their seats.

The winning hare was crowned champion. A shimmering ice medal in the shape of a snowflake was placed around its neck before it hopped a lap of honor around the stadium to the sound of thousands of feet stamping in celebration.

Thunder and Katy walked slowly back toward their friends, heads lowered in shame. It wasn't their fault. They'd tried their best—what more could they do? Now it was up to Cassandra and Zia to turn their fortunes around.

CHAPTER SEVEN

❄ ❄ ❄ ❄ ❄ ❄ ❄ ❄ ❄

Cassandra was amazing at swimming, but she was also shy and hated performing in front of other people. Even street dancing, which she was equally good at and loved, she preferred doing alone in her bedroom. Katy and Zia reminded her that it was the taking part, not the winning, that mattered. But one of them had to win today if they were going to join the festivities. They squeezed their hands together tightly before Cassandra walked away. They hoped she would be OK.

A huge cavern had opened up in the icy ground, exposing an Olympic-sized swimming pool, and Cassandra and her fellow competitors—two seals, a walrus, a narwhal, an orca whale, and a dolphin—had a lane each. Cassandra, now shivering in just a thin undershirt and leggings, stood on the side with the seals and the walrus, while the other animals waited in the water for the race to begin.

A polar bear smaller than Pilar lumbered up to the start line and shouted for the swimmers to get ready. Cassandra stepped forward so just her toes were peeking over the edge of the pool, then crouched down with her arms outstretched in a diving position. When the whistle went, she was first to dive into the water, but she immediately came up gasping for air while the other animals began to race. Within moments, she'd dragged herself back to the edge of the pool and out onto the side.

"It must be freezing in there!" Zia exclaimed, concerned that her friend would catch pneumonia. "It isn't fair. Pilar knows we don't have blubber or fur to keep us warm."

They ran from their seats and sprinted over to a wet and now very shivery Cassandra, just as the whistle was blown to signal the end of the race. The orca had won and was swimming celebratory laps of the pool while the crowd went wild again, stamping their feet and beating their wings.

"Does anyone have a towel?" shouted Zia.

"Quick, our friend's freezing!" yelled Katy.

The small polar bear with the whistle plodded over and took Cassandra in a bear hug, wrapping her up and rubbing her down like an enormous fluffy bath towel. Then it plodded off without saying a word, leaving Cassandra wide-eyed with shock.

"Did I really just get a hug from a polar bear?" she asked, forcing herself to smile through chattering teeth. "I'm sorry about the race, by the way. The water was just too cold. My body went into shock!"

"It's not your fault," said Zia with a sympathetic shrug.

"And it's not like you did any worse than me in the high jump!" added Katy.

"Or me," said Thunder. "It's just that we're all good at different things—and in snow and ice we're not as good as the animals who live here."

"I need to get going," said Zia, pointing to the four enormous polar bears warming up with weights made of huge blocks of ice.

"Break a leg!" said Thunder.

"Yes, good luck!" encouraged Katy and Cassandra.

I'm going to need it, Zia thought, as she walked away from her friends. There was no way she'd be able to beat four polar bears in a weightlifting contest. What were they thinking?

The first block of ice she was asked to lift was so heavy that, no matter how much she strained and heaved, she couldn't budge it even a bit. The four polar bears, on the other hand, were able to lift it with a single paw. Zia had to admit defeat before she'd even started, much to the amusement of the bears and the crowd. But she wasn't ready to go home yet. *Think, think…* She searched her brain to come up with a solution. And as the last weight was lifted and the biggest polar bear was crowned champion, she had an idea. She held her breath as she rummaged around in her rucksack, wishing hard for the things they'd need. When she saw them appear, she zipped the bag shut again in disbelief. She didn't think it would work! Zia decided to keep them as a surprise for her friends—then she ran over, filled with nervous excitement.

"Zia, you lost! Why are you looking so happy?" asked Katy.

"Because I have a plan! Listen, Pilar and her council *knew* we wouldn't win any of those games. Don't you see—every animal we've been up against is designed to cope with the challenges of snow and ice, unlike us. We were never going to win!"

"OK, but how does that help?" asked Cassandra. She was back in her Arctic explorer coat and holding it snuggly around her body to keep warm.

"Because we need to remember why we're here," continued Zia excitedly. "To discover more about the Arctic and the animals who are *perfectly designed* to live here."

Her friends still looked on blankly.

"Listen, I've been thinking about this. If we can get Pilar to agree to one last contest, one that all the animals who competed today take part in too, including us, we might be able to stay. Trust me!"

She just hoped she was right—that her plan was really going to work.

CHAPTER EIGHT

✳ ✳ ✳ ✳ ✳ ✳ ✳ ✳ ✳

Pilar approached slowly, the wolf, walrus, and eagle standing behind her in a line.

"On behalf of the council, we'd like to thank you for competing in our games today. For a cat and three humans, you don't lack courage! But now you must return home. Farewell."

"Um, P-Pilar...p-please, we have one more request." Zia knew that if she didn't speak now, she'd lose her nerve. "I know we didn't win today, but we'd like to challenge you to one last contest—if you agree, of course."

Pilar scratched her head. "I'm listening," she said brusquely.

Zia breathed out. "What we have in mind could teach *all* of us an important lesson. Three rounds, like a triathlon. We'll start with a swim, then the high jump and end with an obstacle race. If anyone fails to finish one of the three stages, that person or animal is out and can't continue to the next round."

Pilar scratched her head again and went to speak to the wolf, eagle, and walrus standing behind her. She returned with the same curious grin Zia had seen her wearing earlier. "You have a deal," she said, shaking Zia's hand with her paw. "We never turn down a contest."

"I *knew* it!" Zia said triumphantly after Pilar had left them alone. "Now we'll *definitely* get to stay for the festivities!"

"But I still don't understand how we're going to win," sighed Katy.

"Nor me," agreed Cassandra, frowning.

Zia tapped the side of her nose and winked at her friends. "You'll just have to wait and see!"

All the participants were called to the pool first. Zia opened up her bag to pull out the very things she'd wished for. Wet suits! Cassandra and Katy's eyes lit up when they saw them.

"Zia, you're so clever! Now I'm actually going to be able to stay in the water long enough to compete!" Cassie shrieked.

They hurried to put them on—except for

Thunder, who said he looked ridiculous. But soon they were all lining up at the edge of the pool alongside the sea creatures, polar bears, and Arctic hares.

The whistle went. The race started. The water was freezing and still made Zia and the others gasp as they dived off the side, but their wet suits acted like blubber, meaning at least it wasn't now *impossible* to swim. The only contestants who couldn't swim were the hares, who soon gave up and climbed soggily out of the pool. Thunder also struggled—cats HATE water—but managed slowly to kitty paddle himself to the other end. The girls weren't much faster. This time the narwhal won by the tip of its long, sword-like nose. But none of this mattered—the four friends were through to the second event!

Now they were lined up for the high jump and, with the champion hares out of the game, the girls stood far more of a chance. There was one round rather than three this time, and one by one the sea creatures failed to make the jump. They couldn't *walk* on land, let alone *jump* on it—but rules were rules, and if an animal didn't make it over the pole, they were disqualified. Next came the polar bears, but their big paws and bellies made them clumsy. As they heaved themselves awkwardly into the air, only one out of four managed to clear the pole without knocking it off.

Then it was the girls. Cassandra went first but skidded badly and couldn't launch herself high enough.

Next came Zia, who almost made it but whose long braid caught around the pole and pulled it off. Then it was Katy's turn. She jumped higher than any of the girls had jumped that day—the pole wobbled dangerously but stayed put! *She was through!* Last it was Thunder's turn. He cleared the height easily and, without the hares competing, was by far the best jumper left in the competition.

"So far everything's going to plan!" whispered Zia happily, as Katy, Thunder, and one large polar bear were left to tackle the final event.

"GOOD LUCK KATY AND THUNDER!" shouted Cassandra and Zia from their arena seats.

The obstacles were all made of shimmering blue ice. There was a giant block of ice to climb over, followed by floating stepping stones positioned in a sort of "S" across the pool, and finally the competitors would have to make their way through an ice tunnel to reach the finish line.

When the whistle blew, the three contestants took off, the polar bear in the lead as soon as they were out of the starting blocks. He made it over the first obstacle without difficulty, followed by Thunder, then Katy. Then he leapt effortlessly across the pool with enormous strides.

Katy and Thunder crossed more cautiously, Katy's stones wobbling furiously as she landed on each of them, but they were soon both safely on the other side too.

The final obstacle was the ice tunnel and, as the bear approached, now even further in the lead, Zia noticed his expression change. He tried to push himself through but the more he tried, the more he seemed to wedge himself tightly in the hole.

"Do you think he's stuck?" asked Cassandra worriedly, as Thunder and Katy caught up with the bear.

The girls watched Katy try to find a way past until eventually she gave up and bent down to whisper something in Thunder's ear. He winked at her then squeezed his way through the bear's thick legs. Seconds later, Thunder was out the other side of the tunnel, running as fast as he could toward the finish line.

CHAPTER NINE

❄ ❄ ❄ ❄ ❄ ❄ ❄ ❄ ❄

A team of animals with axes and ropes charged into the arena to free the still-wedged bear. The girls and Thunder also rushed over and gathered round, anxious the polar bear might be stuck inside forever. It took some digging and pulling but suddenly the bear shot from the tunnel like a cork from a bottle. As soon as it was free, Thunder was presented with his winner's medal to rapturous applause. Even the polar bear went over to shake his paw.

"Thunder, you did it, you did it!" cried Katy, holding her cat above her head in celebration.

"Katy, please put me down," Thunder grumbled, not used to the attention. "Anyway, don't you mean, *we* did it?"

Cassandra nodded. "We couldn't have done it without Zia's idea. How did you *know*, Zia?"

"It was just something Thunder said. That we're all good at different things." She grinned. "It occurred to me that he's right and we're all talented in different ways."

They stopped chatting then because Pilar was coming over with her fellow council members.

"Congratulations," the polar bear said with a deep chuckle. The atmosphere between the bear and the girls was friendlier now, less suspicious. "You've impressed us today. You've showed tremendous determination. But you said you wanted to teach us an important lesson. Please, explain."

"It's simple really." Zia felt her insides swell with pride. "Arctic animals are adapted for life on snow and ice, but their abilities are shaped by the world around them. An animal may be good at swimming, but that's no use if it has to move on land. An animal may be great at jumping, but that's no use if it has to travel in water. This competition has made me realize that *every* habitat is important, because *every creature* needs their *own habitat* to survive!"

Pilar's grin widened and for the first time Zia didn't feel scared of the bear.

"You're right. That is a valuable lesson." She chuckled again, her big belly bouncing up and down. "And you've taught us that not all humans are bad!" She winked and then presented them with three more snowflake-shaped ice medals like the one that hung around Thunder's neck.

"You've all earned these. Wear them well," she said, placing them over the girls' heads, "and always remember the things humans can do to protect the Arctic. You see, if more humans—courageous and intelligent humans like you—truly understand the damage being done to our planet and try to do something about it, the world might begin to heal. Did you know that burning fossil fuels such as oil and gas is one of the biggest causes of climate change, because of the amount of carbon dioxide released into the atmosphere? This is why the ice caps are disappearing and with them the homes of the animals you see around you. How would humans like it if their homes starting melting away?"

The girls hung their heads.

"So the more people you tell about this, the more chance we have of reversing the Great Melt. Now come," said Pilar, changing the mood with a warm smile. "It's time to eat. This has been a truly special winter games!"

The girls and Thunder followed Pilar back through the frozen archway, where in front of them hundreds of animals were sitting around the biggest picnic blanket Zia had ever seen. The blanket was made of ice, with delicate snowflakes engraved upon its surface that glittered and twinkled like stars. But it's what covered the blanket that excited the girls the most: the finest spread of food they'd ever seen. There were snowflake-shaped sandwiches, cakes with blue icing, donuts with blue and silver frosting, and, most amazing of all, mountains and mountains of silvery-blue ice cream!

"A North Pole picnic!" squealed Zia, smiling at her friends. "We get to have our picnic after all!"

Cassandra, Katy, and Thunder beamed and looked as eager as Zia to start eating.

"Please, help yourselves," Pilar said kindly.

"Oh, we brought some things too!" said Zia, suddenly remembering the emergency snacks they'd packed for their adventure. She reached into her rucksack and pulled out the chocolate bars and candy to share with their new friends.

Pilar nodded in approval, and they all dived in, loading their plates to the brim. Only when they couldn't fit anything else in their stomachs, Zia turned to Pilar.

"Thank you, for everything," she said, swallowing her final mouthful. "We'll never forget our trip to the Arctic, or you, or this picnic. How can we ever thank you?"

Pilar smiled. "The lesson we've learned is a great place to start." She gestured to all the animals around them. "Our differences need to be celebrated. And every homeland needs our protection. *This* is what you need to think about and take home to your friends and family. Will you do that for me? For all of us?"

"We will, we promise," the girls said together.

"I'll make certain they will!" Thunder added, trying to make himself useful.

Everything Pilar had told them chimed exactly with what Ms. Coco had taught them about the responsibility we have as humans to protect our planet. Seeing the North Pole melting for themselves,  and knowing these animals were at real risk of losing their habitat, made the girls even more determined to share this message with the world.

"Remember our class at school," Zia said, turning to Katy and Cassandra, "when we talked about the things we can do to help combat climate change?"

"Like using less energy?" Cassandra asked.

"Exactly," said Zia. "Simple things, really, like walking or cycling to school rather than taking the car, which burns gasoline and releases harmful gases into the atmosphere."

"Or turning lights off when we leave a room, so we use less electricity?" offered Katy.

"Yes, and turning the TV off rather than leaving it on standby," said Zia.

"How about eating less meat?" asked Cassandra. "I'm sure I remember learning that cows release methane from their bottoms!"

"Oh yes, that's right!" said Zia. "The more

cows that are farmed, the more methane in the atmosphere. And too much methane also causes climate change!"

"There's recycling too, of course," said Katy. "If we reuse and recycle, less energy is needed to make things in the first place. And there's a lot less waste!"

"You've got it!" said Pilar, listening in to their conversation. "There really is *so* much you can do."

"Don't forget equal rights for animals," offered Thunder seriously.

Katy grinned, then ruffled Thunder's head. "I'll tell that to the next mouse or bird you catch in the yard, shall I?"

Everyone laughed.

"It's good to know not *all* humans are intent on destroying our planet." Pilar smiled gratefully. "And if you can share these thoughts with others, there might be a chance to turn the planet's fortunes around. Now, are you ready to say goodbye?"

They all nodded their heads slowly, while Pilar pulled them into a warm bear hug. They felt sad to leave, but it really was time to go— they had an important job to do! When Pilar released them, the girls moved into a circle, Thunder in the middle, and held each other's hands. Then they squeezed their eyes tightly closed.

"Now, repeat after me: I wish to go home," said Pilar.

"*I wish to go home,*" they said together.

In an instant, electricity started pulsing through their bodies. They felt hot, then cold, then hot again, like their insides were filled with bubbles. When at last those feelings had passed, they opened their eyes.

They were still standing in a circle, only now they were surrounded by white sheets and duvets rather than soft, powdery snow. Outside it was dark, snowflakes falling and settling on the windowsill, and Thunder was meowing and cleaning his ears with his paw.

"It happened again!" Katy said, swishing her ponytail round as she looked down at her normal clothes.

"Hey, look!" Cassandra was holding a small silver snowflake in the palm of her hand. "The medal—I think it's shrunk!"

"I know what that is!" cried Zia, examining her own tiny medal. "It's a charm—like the star we brought home from the Wishing Star. Don't you see? We can add these to our bracelets, and they'll remind us of the lesson we learned at the North Pole!"

They helped each other secure the snowflake

charms to their bracelets, while Katy helped fix Thunder's to his collar.

"Where to next?" asked Zia.

"It's your turn for a playdate, Cassie. Any ideas?" Katy asked.

Cassandra thought for a moment. "I do, but it's going to be a surprise." She grinned.

"Not even a clue?" asked Zia.

"Let's just say, we might need swimming things again!" Cassandra laughed.

"Amazing!" Katy clapped her hands, although Thunder didn't look so pleased.

Zia paused for a second, thinking about everything they'd been through and everything they'd just learned. She took her friends' hands in her own.

"As long as we're together," she said, "I really don't mind."

How to Plan Your Own
Playdate Adventure

1. Decide where you would like to go on your adventure.

2. Plan how you would get there. Do you need to build anything or imagine yourself in a new land?

3. Imagine what exciting or challenging things might happen on your adventure.

4. Decide if you are going to learn anything from your adventure.

5. Most important of all, remember to have fun!

THE ARCTIC

✳ ✳ ✳ ✳ ✳ ✳ ✳ ✳ ✳

Did you know…?

The Arctic around the North Pole is mostly ocean. However, at its center are polar ice caps—dome-shaped sheets of ice that form because polar regions receive less heat from the sun than other areas of the Earth's surface.

An Arctic summer has daylight twenty-four hours a day and is a time for polar animals to feed. In winter, when more of the ocean freezes and the land is covered in a thick layer of snow, the animals have adapted to keep warm and survive. Some hibernate, such as the Arctic squirrel, and some, such as the Arctic tern, migrate to warmer climates.

Unfortunately, average temperatures at the poles have begun to rise in recent years due to changes in the environment. As temperatures rise, the polar ice caps start to melt and break apart. NASA satellite photographs show that the polar ice caps are shrinking 9% every ten years.

As ice disappears, so does the habitat of polar animals.

.

A number of human activities have led to climate change. These are:

* Burning fossil fuels, such as oil and gas.
* An increase in cattle farming. There are over 1.5 billion cows in the world releasing methane into the atmosphere!
* Deforestation. The rise in demand for beef has led to a rise in deforestation to create more land for the cattle to roam in and to

grow the crops that feed them. As the forests are destroyed, carbon dioxide levels rise, which traps heat from the sun and causes temperatures to rise further.

There are a number of things we can all do to try to help combat climate change:

* Walk, cycle, or scoot to your destination rather than going by car.
* If you can, take a train rather than a plane.
* Use less power at home. Remember to switch lights off when you leave a room and turn off your television rather than leaving it on standby.
* Get electricity from renewable sources like wind and sun instead of coal and other fossil fuels that need to be burned to release energy.
* Reuse and recycle as much as you can.
* Plant more trees.
* Eat less meat.

* Take action! Talk to people about the dangers of climate change, start a petition, write to your local governing body and encourage them to push for regulations that will support our planet.

Emma Beswetherick is the mother of two young children and wanted to write exciting, inspirational, and enabling adventure stories to share with her daughter. Emma is a publisher with Little, Brown and lives in south-west London with her family and two ragdoll cats, one of whom was the inspiration for Thunder. *The Wishing Star* was her first book.

Anna Woodbine is an independent book designer and illustrator based in the hills near Bath, England. She works on all sorts of book covers from children's to adult's, classics to crime, memoirs to meditation. She takes her tea with a dash of milk (Earl Grey, always), loves the wind in her face, comfortable shoes, and that lovely damp smell after it's rained.

Find her at: thewoodbineworkshop.co.uk

If you loved this story, then you will love:

THE WISHING STAR

Katy, Cassie, and Zia find themselves transported into outer space when their rocket made out of recycled waste magically becomes life-sized.

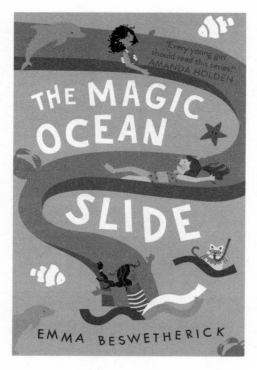

THE MAGIC OCEAN SLIDE

Katy, Cassie, Zia, and Thunder discover an underwater world and learn there is more to the ocean than meets the eye!

THE GIANT CHESTNUT

Transported into an enchanted forest, the girls are surprised that the further they go, the fewer trees there seem to be.